Charles Leonard Moore

A Book of Day-dreams

Charles Leonard Moore

A Book of Day-dreams

ISBN/EAN: 9783337736439

Printed in Europe, USA, Canada, Australia, Japan

Cover: Foto ©Andreas Hilbeck / pixelio.de

More available books at **www.hansebooks.com**

A BOOK OF DAY-DREAMS

BY

CHARLES LEONARD MOORE

SECOND EDITION REVISED

NEW YORK
HENRY HOLT AND COMPANY
1892

ESS,

I.

NAKED December have I curtained out,
Its cobweb branches crossing the cold sky ;—
Dead am I to the hurrying flakes about,
Dead and close-tombed in Eastern luxury.
But not the fire's rich rapture with itself,
The carpet's glow, the painted air above,
The gleam of red-clad volumes from the shelf,
The stainèd chessmen or yon shadowy glove,
The mantel's romance of bronze-mailèd knights,
The sometime showing fresco pastoral,
The curtains closing me with these delights
Deep, deep, unfathomably out of call,
    Not these, but dreams and reveries allowed
    Make me o'er all Time's empty triumphs proud.

II.

Love, Melancholy, Mirth, the lyric three,
Youth's myrmidons, are with their leader flown,
Or if they linger, linger doubtfully,
Like halting guests upon the threshold stone ;
Like birds that in the altered forests now
Ominously listen to the winds that blow,
And fear to sing, lest they should shake some bough
Laden with airy imminence of snow.
But not for aye my life so blank is made,
An inventory of oblivion ;
In hours like this, the dance-inwoven braid
Of dreams moves by me and I mount a throne ;
   Then do I barter all the world for this,
   To think my dreams real, real the bliss.

III.

Then in my hand I hold the master-trick,
Having and Hope are then alike in hue,
Joy's lightning issue then that breathes so quick
Drags out infinity with processional view ;
Then Honor straying from the courts of men
Comes to me all content, and Peace with her
Sets the lost Pleiad in the sky again
Till the round girdle blazes without blur ;
Then do the fabrics of the world rebuild
In the clear day of my transparent rhyme,
Then Spring does flush, and Autumn overgild,
And Winter carve the lines I leave to time ;
    Then my heart rushes forth to meet its lot,
    Then is the face of woman without blot.

IV.

Throng-summoning sleep, I need thee not at all,
Nor Morphia, nor the wine-cup's drowsèd steam,
Nor even the poet's page imperial,
To link my daylight to a world of dream ;
Yet, dread enchanters of intelligence,
Stroke my eyes, too, with your wing-budded wands,
So my soul, loosed, may make its voyage hence,—
Soul unappeased at rumor of more lands,—
And find, perhaps, the passage to the East,
And tranquil isles, and days of tropic bloom,
Or if its quest be vain, itself increased,
Know its own stature equal to its doom :
    Eternally open the sky's line does flit,
    But only death and dreams do pierce through it.

V.

When I do count the centuries that bar
Love's most perfected vision from my arms,
When I behold the shapes that current are
And make compare with age-long buried charms,
Alone enamored of the vanishèd,
Musing on shadows I would woo to sense,
I write upon the earth that seemeth dead
The epitaph of every excellence.
Then comes some dream to lift Life's dusky pall,
To body forth Juliet balconied,
To bring again Antony's admiral,
To make all real expectancy did read,
　　To make me hear my dreamèd lady's breath
　　And look upon her rescued eyes of death.

VI.

Better perfection mocking thee afar,
Better eluding footfalls in the air,
Better the hope and worship of a star,
Than the home-bringing of the fairest fair.
Joy may make wild, content may lull each sense,
Earth be twice windowed in thy lady's eyes,
But the day comes, and the intelligence,—
The ghastly horror of a chill surmise,—
When shall thy love in all her glittering shows
Gauds, raiments, actions innocent or rash,
Seem like the Magi's figure of a rose,
Reflowering ghostlike from its pallid ash,
 Or like the writing that a space entire
 Gleams on the black, curled paper in the fire.

VII.

The action of the most heroic deed
Is scarce distinguishable from an ague fit :
Man in Life's stream is like a shaken reed,—
Silent for all the river's mouthing it ;
Nothing does he reveal, and nothing keep
(Ranked ghost-like beckoner to the crinkling sedge),
Of the stream's purpose, flowing strong and deep
Past his vague motions in its lapping edge.
I hear the foreign echoes from the street,—
Faint sounds of revel, traffic, conflict keen,
And think that man's reiterated feet
Have gone such ways since e'er the world has been :
   I wonder how each oft-used tone and glance
   Retains its might and old significance.

VIII.

Earth's rocks, in orderèd succession ranged,
Are made by Time's impression different;
Being mutability, man bears unchanged
The mark of every age's accident,
So that all long-past shapes do seem to come
In a mistaken habit of to-day,
And each contemporary is at home
Within the crumbled towers of hoar decay ;
And thence is Fame's eternal audience,
Which does applaud itself in antique shows,
And at Time's circle-mirror burns intense,
Reacting each anticipated pose :
　　Thy smile, thy gesture unto Pharaoh known,
　　Outlives its presentation carved in stone.

IX.

Soon is the echo and the shadow o'er,
Soon, soon we lie with lid-encumbered eyes,
And the great fabrics that we reared before
Crumble to make a dust to hide who dies.
Gone, and the empty and unstatued air
Keeps not the mold or gesture of our limbs,
But doth with its investiture repair
And fold what next unto its circle swims.
Fools, so to paint our pageant grave with deeds,
And make division in the elements ;
Earth yields us splendid mansions for our needs,
And only takes our lives to pay the rents.
  Ah, but our dreams !   Beyond earth's count they rise
  In sage and hourly eternities.

X.

These words, that slow, plashed rains obliterate,
Writ and rewrit, have tired the touch of Time ;
These passions that my heart does deem so great
Are plagiaries remembering some old rhyme :
Ay, this inheritance of moving flesh,
Pieced from the shreds and dust of antique men,
Does its old deeds in the old ways afresh,
Checked oft by the familiar doubt, " Again ! "
But my soul is not second-hand, nor staled
The sure, proud visions surging through my heart ;
New, new they rise, their glory has not failed
Before, nor shall a second time upstart ;
    God, wanting my consent, shall not create
    The world within me where I rule as fate.

XI.

What binds us to the world ?   Deep sounds and gleams
We find or feign in it.   But it can be
Most subtle in its forgery of dreams,
And borrows from us to our beggary.
What else ?   The hint of conscience in the heart
That still shows frankness for its own proud sake,
And, though unasked thrust in a world of art,
Still nobly keeps the vow it did not make.
What more ?   Ah, most the pleasure of the eye,
The touch of bosoms mutinously fair,
Kisses, those last heirs of reality,
And the soul-lingering loops of perfumed hair,—
   These keep us from Elysium.   O, my soul,
   Break their slight chain, escape their strong control !

XII.

Dreams must forego the good that doing has,
Strife's glow and grace and olive guerdon won,
Joys that have wings, but still like swallows pass
Close to the ground, deeds done or well begun.
Too vast Thought's domain for such limit joys,
Daylight may dawn and die unnoticed there,
And the soul, soaring from life's safe employs,
Is but a traveler in that upper air ;—
Traveler forthright, athwart, in blinded path,
Seeking to wrest Time's secret from Time's rule,
To give to nature more than nature hath,—
Problem divine for every noble fool.

    Look you at what this crucible does hold,—
    How the lead bubbles with the rose of gold.

XIII.

Now is the hour of uncertainties,
As changeling stars and Midnight's glancing eye
Do work upon the herded waves increase,
So in me swell the tides of mystery.
Where Morn with rose appareled, white impearled,
Rose from her bed of bridal with the Sea,
Gapes the enormous entrance of some world
Where, our own founders, fragmentarily,
Earth's shows and that new nature built by men,
Our near, birth-giving, home-proved, age-known sods,
Fade, and our fixed foundations melt, and then
Pale Dominations exile our hearth gods :
   Yet though we compass lack and stars be few,
   Up anchor, Soul, and " Courage " cry thy crew.

XIV.

From adoration learn I to deny,
As amid music snaps the o'erstrainèd wire,
For overlearnèd grows the loving eye,
And too desirous even in desire.
Deep in the secret heart in sudden lair
The imperious image of our hope does sit,
And portrait after portrait for compare
We handle, but the features do not fit.
Soul unto soul glooms darkling and unknown,
Kisses but seal the truce of enemies,
No voice finds echo in another's tone,
And the heart still for its true fellow cries.
    Naked thou strainest a bride unto thy breast,
    But in dreams only is she all possessed.

XV.

Disguise upon disguise, and then disguise,
Equivocations at the rose's heart,
Life's surest pay a poet's forgeries,
The gossamer gold coinage of our art.
Why hope for truth ?   Thy very being slips,
Lost from thee, in thy crowd of masking moods.
Why hope for love ?   Between quick-kissing lips
Is room and stage for all hate's interludes.
One with thy love thou art !—her eyes, her hair
Known to thy soul, a pure estate of bliss ,
But some least motion, look, or changèd air,
And nadir unto zenith nearer is :
    Thou mayest control her limbs, but not begin
    To know what planet rules the tides within.

XVI.

War I then 'gainst the strong edicts of Love
And all the ages' purple-dyed report ?
No, by the heavens in the depths whereof
Is Love's inviolable and perfect court !
Tiptoe for flight and yet not fugitive,
On my heart's height and verge Love ever stands,
With eyes that conquer Fate, with lips that give
Fevers to Death, with fame-awarding hands : ·
The secret that upon her face is born,
The music of the motion of her limbs,
Are an empoisoned madness.   I pass on,
Mute questioner of the heavens' empty rims,
   As one who, with the sunset on his face,
   Turns to match colors in some darkened place.

XVII.

Thus would I charge my soul.   Go thou and float
With her I love in thought-unclouded play
On the world's naked pathway far remote,
Leaving this dull encampment of the day,
Till the mysterious stars and symbol lights—
Dragon, or bear, or lion, as they chance—
Shall alter, and the heaven resume by rights
Its inner and immortal countenance :
For floating on that breast of Time will be
Time's secret, our two selves, loosed from all task,
Divided, yet one strong identity ;
And at the sight all shows must straight unmask,
   And throughout space one pulse of joy must leap
   To wed light with the wandering, obscure deep.

XVIII.

O most pure spirit and subtle being of force,
Dream beyond thought and God beyond all dream,
Why hast thou set thine absolute divorce
Between the separate souls that from thee stream ?
Earth's corporate figures each in each may blend
And take each other's image and impress,
Coupled with shadow till the world does end.
But sole the spirit lives, and shadowless,
Unknown its seat, and all its act in doubt,
Its immortal being to itself most strange.
How can it mingle with the world without,
It the one certain thing that shall not change ?
   This is its doom : to be, O fate perverse,
   Prisoned at heart of the free universe.

XIX.

This is the horror of man's glorious mood,—
Self-sphered, self-poised, by nought without possessed,—
To seek with certain aim its single good,
Each shrill voice differing from the choric rest.
Harsh law, yet well !   Else would the death of one
Poison the goblets of life's general feast,
Else would the myriad world's unending moan
Be in each ear aye iterate and increased.
The image of a star in every soul
Lives, and does draw its charge athwart, apart ;
Together does the pageant seem to roll ;
But, ah ! the distance, the unneighbored heart :
    Stars may not meet till they in ruin end,
    And, save in death, no soul may know a friend.

XX.

Yet if uncaring for the increasing ghosts
That throng and beckon where life's paths descend,
In turn uncared for by the human hosts,
The soul may lean on Nature as a friend.
Look in her eyes : those shadowed realms are fair.
Cling, closer cling to her deep-cloven breast :
Her cool arms thrill, her eyes do seem to wear
The very secret of the sweetest rest.
Sink, sink to sleep, so choosing to believe
Thou hast a balm for all the hurt without,
A consolation for the thoughts that grieve,
An answer to the unconquerable doubt.
  Day shall wait on thee, and the twilight pale,
  The stars shall thicken and the leaves shall fail.

XXI.

Fool ! so deluded in thine own great lot,
Nature can succor not thy mysteries :
She is immortal, but may enter not
The hollow circle where thy being lies.
Rose-hedges, ridged horizons, and her ring,
Of azure keeps thee ; ay, thy flesh is built
Up from her infinite environing,—
Sounds, motions, scents ; yet sudden if thou wilt
Empties this empire and the soul remains,
The soul swift, splendid, daring, competent,—
Neither uppropped by Nature, nor in chains,—
Doubting alone the errand it was sent :
   Perchance that dew-wet branch that swished my face
   Helped form my soul ; but I, I knew its grace.

XXII.

No bloom breaks from the marbles of the past,
Blurred is the picture of the present act,
Hope's dim inheritance, in the future cast,
Bears not a harvest through the shadowy tract.
Oh, dulled with Memory and tired with Hope,
Dwellers on earth, a new, sweet faith I bring,—
A magic that shall lift the heaviest cope,
A medicine that shall mend each broken wing !
Say, art thou rich, haggard with weight of gold,
Yet always wanting what thou canst not name ?
Say, art thou poor, an outcast from the fold ?
Equal my power in thee, my word the same :
  'This must thou do ; wrap thyself round in dreams
  And scorn the presence of the world that seems.

XXIII.

Fortune, proud fool ! that deemest the hearts of men
Waked and won only by thy slight allure,
Know that thy footstep seals those founts again
That else were free, that else were full and pure :
Thou hast Life's keys, and dost command success,—
Success, poor shadow of the soul of hope ;
But all thy gain is present weariness
And the gods' laughter from their unscaled slope.
Go, harlot, with thy faces of regard,
Wind-varying for the lovers at thy side,
I am not poor enough for thy reward,
Honor and splendor in my heart abide ;
    I want thee not, save that thou kneel, and so
    Proffer thy service as cup-bearers do.

XXIV.

For me the dark within, girdled with fires, ·
Thought-fashioned or self-lit ere thought began,
Filled with sinister stir that still retires,
The echoes in the lonely heart of man ;
For me the brink of death, the abyss of fear,
The trysting-place of madness and of ruth,
Where joy and hope and love begin, and where
Opens the only road that leads to truth ;
Where thronèd dwells my being's subtle king,
Half maker of the deeds he must rehearse,
The imperious and unweariable thing,
Thought, set in his own forgèd universe.
    Doubt though he may, I doubt not him, but come
    And, unreluctant, charge him with my doom.

XXV.

Oh, answerer to all unspoken needs,
Nurse of the soul's faint flame and secret breath,
Muse of most mighty arts and of those deeds
That do not go the usual way to death,
Dæmon I call thee, guardian who doth stand,
Torch-bearing and with glorious guiding eyes,
'Twixt those dark chasms on the either hand,
The greater and the less infinities !
Take thou my heart's blood, that our league may lack
No sign to make me thine and keep me so ;
What thou dost bid I do and hold not back ;
Then, then, one hour of joy do thou bestow :
  Thronged are my heavens or their aisles unfilled,
  As thy sweet music whispers or is stilled.

XXVI.

Come, gossip of the eternal true antique,
Dumb art thou of the undescended One,
But of the lesser godheads may'st thou speak,
Their dynasty does not outdate thine own ;
So if I think of colors thou wilt fling
Hyperion's shadow on my narrowed eyes,
And if I dream of music, thou wilt bring
Lutes that still hold the Muses' memories ;
Thou wilt the thin, sparse chronicles of old
Fill with all fortunate figures of bright youth,
Thou wilt regild Apollo's hair of gold,
And move the lips oracular of truth ;
    Thou wilt reshrine the earliest god of love,
    And make my heart the altar-fire thereof.

XXVII.

Dæmon, O Dæmon, thou lute-playing fiend,
For lust of love thou hast my soul in fee :
I am thy slave ; but for this cause demeaned,
The whole world else knows no such royalty ;
Thou hast my soul : see that thou yield instead
A distillation past the rose's bloom,
Hues that shall strike the sunset's colors dead,
Shades subtler than the closely-shuttled gloom ;
Divide each joy, dive to each spirit-sense,
And build dominion in an atom's space,
Make sure the heavens with starry permanence,
Ay, carve in marble mystery's mocking face.
    Do this and we are quits ; but less, thou art
    Falser than the false world from which I part.

XXVIII.

After our argument and doctrine proved
Of the earth's show and senses counterfeit,
Do not thou cheat me, O, my one beloved :
Be thou my life and all my world complete.
Ages of shadow have refined thy face,
Thy limbs are woven of dusk and filmy dyes,
Thine eyes build from the dark, but have no place,—
Dim counter stars of crossed nativities ;
But thou hast ventured where no foot has trod,
Scarce can'st thou silence all thy thunderous past ;
In the first circle that was drawn by God
Thy being rose and was not thence outcast.
    Now in this narrow cell thou feignest to be,
    Who art afloat upon the eternal sea !

XXIX.

That which shall last for aye can have no birth.
Thou art immortal ! therefore thou hast been
A voyage to which the journey of the earth
Is but the shifting of some tawdry scene.
Thou wert not absent when the camp began
Of the great captains of the middle air,—
Sirius and Vega and Aldeberan,—
Myriads, and but the marshals numbered there ;
Ay, earlier yet in the God-purposed void,
The dream and desert of oblivion,
Thou livedest,—a thought of one to be employed
Ere yet Time's garments thou did'st take and don :
    Guest that no footprint on my threshold leaves,
    Speak, O, dim traveler, speak : thy host believes !

XXX.

Aerial tenant under umbered eaves,
Thou tresspasser on Twilight's ancient homes,
One word of thine—and earth no more deceives ;
Three steps with thee—and all the future comes ;
Holding thy robe, I sink to that last house,
The mind's deep hollow where the Muses hide,
And couched upon the poignant-breathed fir-boughs,
Accept the wide-eyed phantoms at thy side.
Dell above dell, but nowhere the domed sky,
Trees girdling darkness and themselves obscure,
Lanes slanting to oblivion's mystery,—
This is thy realm, thrice guarded and secure ;

   This is our stage on which we may enact
   Life's secret dream and undivulged act.

XXXI.

Sometimes I image thee a beauteous youth,
Stained with bright blood and blushes through and through,
Gay in the service of austerest truth,
In borrowed beauty, Beauty set to woo ;
The panoply of maiden youth is worn
Then on my heart, true love-knots, gaudy ties,
And silver buckles and lace sleeves half-torn,
All rash inconsequent and headlong guise :
Yet I am better when thou thus art by,
And wiser for thy hot blood, generous wars :
Out of thy holy eyes that cannot lie
I read the steady promise of the stars.
    Sleep ever in my breast, sleep within call,
    O armed soldier archangelical !

XXXII.

Sometimes an older comrade dost thou seem,
Wise with the practice of life's dangerous art,
Below the bottom hast thou dived, yet deem
No whit the worse of life or man's poor part :
Within some tavern's cool recess we sit
And watch the garish actors of the day,
Who, as outside they seem to stage our wit,
Seek plaudits from the authors of the play ;
Or, turning to our wine, we make debate
Of good and evil, of the turn of chance,
Of the last whisper thou hast had from Fate,
And of my soul's proud soaring dominance.
    Gentle in all thou art, for thou hast seen
    High heaven, and hell, and all the road between.

XXXIII.

And oft dost thou usurp a woman's eyes,
Stars that my gloomy soul keeps safe, when I,
Lost inmate of the oldest paradise,
Feel suddenly flung ope the gate whereby
Love comes, and clear again my way is made
To the harmonious meadows of desire,
Where, mid eternal dawns that cannot fade,—
A burning shadow at the heart of fire,—
Crowned with pure flowers, naked yet unknown,
Thou sittest, and the inviolable secrecy
Of self, that keeps men separate as stone,
Melt'st with a glance, and so reveal'st to me,
   Past the sweet shame of sex, that mirroring deep
   Where our two figures in one image sleep.

XXXIV.

Be as thou wilt, thou art my spirit choice
And counterbalance of the world without;
The sea clinks idly through thy linked voice,
Thine eyes displace the stars and bar day out.
Summed each in each, what care we for the might
Of protestations that the earth does make?
As cards are shuffled or as chessmen fight,
Men go about their games, nor know the stake;
Yet could they, closed in the same bounds as now,
Burn their swift way unto that deeper room,
Life's treasure-chamber? Ay, they could—but how?
Dead! They are dead and do not know their doom.
    Leave them unto their grave, sweet guest! Away!
    The great tides wait to bear us to the day.

XXXV.

Tush for the waves ! we bear our charm within.
Tush for the clouds ! the pilot of the skies
Sleeps in the soul where it had origin.
Tush for the toil ! the cleft spray backward flies.
The land we seek is far, is far remote,
But only to the land we leave—that lost
On the new quay soon grates our charmèd boat,
The sail falls in, the unmeasured sea is crossed.
New lands ?   New worlds ?   I spring upon the beach
No stranger, but a native and a son :
I grasp the soil I grew from in my reach,
And of its distance take dominion.
   And from the thick-stemmed shades in pomp descend
   Gods, heroes, helpers, ay, perchance a friend.

XXXVI.

Then shall we see and know the group divine,
The sure immortals of the world's vague throng,
Ceaseless continuers of the purple line,
The equal-sceptred kings of Deed and Song :
From sire to sire to Orpheus and beyond,
Thrilled with the blood of Hector do they come,
Blazoned on eyes believing, eyes too fond
To fail to follow them unto their home.
Hark ! their thin tread out-echoes the vast hosts
That shake the valleys of the globe beneath ;
Their smile is fire ; their eyes (O, subtle ghosts !)
Have waked in me the passion of the Wreath
   Without whose round not heaven itself is bliss,
   Nor immortality immortal is.

XXXVII.

Though I be less than naught, yet not the less
Keats shall step out to greet me from the rest,—
Keats, who himself went still companionless
Save for the golden genius in his breast ;
Who, spite all weakness and all doubt, was led
(Calm lord of life with full possession crowned)
To life's deep haunt, when other poets fled
Fevered or frantic from the holy ground.
Now made the shepherd of the heavenly plains,
Moving with clouds and stars athwart the blue,
Marshaling mysterious herds to happier strains
Than aught Theocritus or Virgil knew,
   Keats shall step forth, by mighty passions moved,—
   The art he cherished and the earth he loved.

XXXVIII.

Then shall I see a giant deity
Rise on the day-appearing pageant's track,
And loose his sounding arrows through the sky
With sudden echo of the string sprung back ;
And suns and circling stars and wandering lights
May dawn, may darken, may decay and die,
But those sped shafts, sent in such angry flights,
Blazing about the halls of Night, shall lie.
Then shalt thou turn and say with pallid lips,—
"That was the shade of mighty Æschylus ;
His intolerable light becomes eclipse,
His fiery eyes shake shadows over us.
    Thunders do gird him !   Yet but list again,—
    Music as soft as slumber-lulling rain."

XXXIX.

Then shall we come on one in that vast realm,
Forever idle mid the full employ;
Darkness sits o'er him as to overwhelm,
And at his knees Light stands like some pure boy.
From such converse what secret has he guessed?
None knows! But this thou say'st: "Amid all strife
He only at the heart of things at rest
Lifts not a hand to turn the wheel of life.
That Shakespeare is," thou sayest in awèd tone.
"Men knew him busy, cheerful, full of mirth;
They did not deem his spirit sat alone,
Judging all beings of an equal birth.
    To the pure centre of his mind's true white
    Life throws its diverse hues that there unite."

XL.

Then shalt thou, Dæmon, my dark eyes assuage
With squeezèd juices of some spirit herb,
And, ended their long earthly vassalage,
Reality shall to the hope reverb;
Then shall the spaces of the empty air
Unroll the riches they so smoothly hid,
And flashing towers and marble frontage there
Shall gleam, and porch and temple and pyramid;
Then shall I see the forms that mirrored are,
Blurred in their being, on the under-earth,
The divine transport of the face of Law,
Wisdom's sad mien, and Number's magic birth,—
    Visions perfected, whose vague, flying gleams
    Vex and perplex us in the place of dreams.

XLI.

The second of the sevenfold spheres these guard,—
An obscure cavern, intricate, wherein
Echo itself is lost beyond reward.
Here enter and emerge whate'er has been,
Or is, or may be,—herds, with trampling roar,
Of stars and suns, and men that come and go,
And the unfathomable dream of more,
All moving, mingling, melting in strange flow.
This is the realm of change and difference,
Of subtle diminution and increase ;
Naught sure, and yet uncertainties intense
Building a world and bending war to peace.
   Here may we stand, and from the unsorted sty
   Take our inheritance as it wanders by.

XLII.

Then do we gain through gates that never close
Gardens of sunlit aspect and serene,
Girdled with summits from whose wreaths of rose
Fall in eternal folds the myriad green.
About are pastoral reaches and great trees
Whose frontage darkens daylight, and amid
The intermingling intricacies of these
Vases and statues and vast steps are hid,—
Stairs that go where none knows, but go not far,
For this is Heaven, and needs no height above,
Whereon ascending or descending are
Ladies, or else in garments subtly wove,
    Or nobly naked and more evident
    Of Beauty's law, whose being they present.

XLIII.

Root of these glades, a fountain gushes up,
Mirroring again the life it gives, its flow
O'erbubbling like an overbrimming cup,
Veining with silver gleam the grass below :
About its rim—brood of the old disguise—
The Lion of the Desert of the Real
Strides, and with sombre flashes in its eyes
Death and all worser terrors does reveal.
Heed not this guard, my guide, but taste and share
The singing water !   Ah, we grow alive !
My flesh, translated to a thing of air,
Spurns at each chain and intellectual gyve ;
   Life on my lips, and in my bosom peace,—
   Joy's fount in this, whence cometh all increase.

XLIV.

Thou beckonest and I dread not to descend!
The waves climb up, but climbs not up my heart
Calm pulsing.   Dimly seen, thine eyes portend
Some change, and lo! the world of form and art
Fades, is effacèd, is a foreign thing,
And Life's true birth, the blazing prodigy,
Fire, girds us: Fire upon the rolling stream,
Fire on the wallèd vistas that I see,
Fire ever, fire alone; leaping Desire!
Fire is my blood and fire thy sombre eyes,
The very shadows of this world are fire,
And its forged forms melt back as they arise;
    And up and down and here again the same
    Love roaring goes with wings that fan the flame.

XLV.

A voice ! Is it a voice ? A sense of ruth
Or joy too mighty to be understood,
The unintelligible cry of Truth,
O'erwhelms and drowns out every other mood ;
And all the single element of Love,
And all the full designs of former spheres,
Die into silence at the next remove.
Dim colloquist, for this thou trainedst my ears
With spirit-murmurs in the days of time,
That to us, standing on the utmost verge,
Truth's music and immeasurable rhyme
Might from the noises and the night emerge.
    Ah ! well that to the image-heated brain
    Truth's fluted notes came first and last remain.

XLVI.

Yet who this even, equal strain can reach
Is but by halting parted from his end.
Triumph to thee, my Dæmon, thou did'st teach
The way and nobly stood'st my spirit's friend.
Now, now the all-desired Vision comes,
The show of Beauty in its hidden heart,
Rest and Decay tracked to their secret homes,
The accounted figure of the shadowy part ;
Darkness and Light are now together grown,
And Order and Disorder strive no more ;
Space real is, but dwindles into One !
Time lives, but lives no After nor Before :
  Dæmon, halt not. Let us sweep on and be
  Lost in the Godhead of Identity.

XLVII.

For one last question do I seek thine eyes :
Honest thou seemest, yet may'st thou choose to cheat,
And by the long way of illusive lies
Read me false knowledge and my soul's defeat.
Steady thou gazest, yet thy clear orbs within
A flickering serpent glimmer seems to grow ;
My adjuration does surprise thy sin ;
Thou hast deceived me—or dost nothing know !
The way we came is not the way, or hap
Thou knew'st no way, but gave the reins to chance,
And with thy glamour bridged each yawning gap,
That I shouldst praise thee and thy fame advance !
   Or do I wrong thee, or but find thee out ?
   Teacher of scorn, thyself hast taught the doubt !

XLVIII.

So : but angelic anger fills thy face,
Thy height is awful, and thy gloom increased,
And with the gesture of a nobler race
Thou break'st the sceptre of my world released.
Slow floats thy figure through my open door,
And through the entry, o'er the threshold led,
I hear thy echoing footsteps slow withdraw,
And I of hope am disinherited.
Or have I made escape, and am I free,
Or worse condemnèd to a narrower cell?
Sure by myself I touch no Deity,
Thou knew'st the password and the sentinel.
   But better so, rather than with thee dwell
   Forever with the o'er-impossible.

XLIX.

Lo ! I unbar my window and fling ope
The gateways of the world of sense again :
A blazon is upon the eastward slope
In which the dark thought has no part or pain ;
Virgin again the Morn so oft enjoyed
Upon the chilly threshold of the earth,
With limbs yet trembling from the colder void,
Waits to be ushered to the fire and mirth.
O enter, and my empty world possess !
O enter, and the phantoms backward roll !
Be a creation to my nothingness,
An incarnation to my shadowy soul !
    But guard thy realm, and fill each vacant space,
    Or the dread Dæmon will return apace.

L.

Before the birth of Spring there comes a time,
Some February day's faint augury,
With something of the Summer's gentle prime,
Rude yet with Winter's unrelinquished sway.
Such charm of doubtful season is there here ;
Spring's green enamel donned too hastily
Lets icicles and frozen buds appear ;
But the bland air is all the breath of May.
Look not again to see such halting act
In the round of the passion-entered year,
Such tame recital of tumultuous fact
From this full song whose midsummer is near.
  Now, Dæmon, waft I thee my last embrace,
  And mourn the vision of thy vanished face.

LI.

But when resistless, royal Spring comes on,
I have no need for thee, no, none at all ;
The distant echo of her herald horn
Swells in my breast and drowns all other call.
The first, faint token of her presence told,
As, grass new-bladed on some margin field,
Arbutus breaking from its leafy mold,
Or crocus peering from some stony shield,
These lay the ghosts that threaten in my thought,
And bid dreams vanish and the senses live,
And bring my bride to me, the Spring, long sought,
Who swears and kisses and is fugitive,—
  Spring, who makes quick the streams and trees and birds
  And puts the eloquence in mortal words.

LII.

The Spring returns ! What matters then that War
On the horizon like a beacon burns,
That Death ascends, man's most desirèd star,
That Darkness is his hope ? The Spring returns !
Triumphant through the wider-arched cope
She comes, she comes, unto her tyranny,
And at her coronation are set ope
The prisons of the mind, and man is free !
And beggar-garbed or over-bent with snows,
Each mortal, long defeated, disallowed,
Feeling her touch, grows stronger limbed, and knows
The purple on his shoulders and is proud.
  The Spring returns ! O madness beyond sense,
  Breed in our bones thine own omnipotence !

LIII.

As air the waves are and the earth as glass.
I see Life's fire-strown seeds, in shuttled flow,
Rise from the darkness, pass, and then repass,
Kindling each other as they come and go.
The herbage hides not its own change from me,
I seek the oak-tree flushing through its scars,
The buried births in torchèd troop I see,
Plain as the nightly Spring-tide of the stars.
Up climbs the fire to bud, to leaf, to bird,
Up to the winged rose quivering in the air,
Up to the finish and Spring's final word,—
Sweet trouble of the rest,—a woman fair,
    Whose eyes do exile Reason and bring in
    Days and the gods he knew not nor could win.

LIV.

Go hence, Philosophy, thou falsest truth,
Thou unrememberèd remembrancer,
Who rakes the ashes o'er the fires of youth,—
Go, for the golden Morning is astir :
Dialectician of the undying dead,
Thy place is with the vaunt and utmost star,
Not here where roses wreathe about the head,
Where mutinous bosoms swell, where kisses are,
Where the moon-lucent limbs of girls gleam through
Their cloud-belongings, where the tides of blood
Follow such sway in turbulent retinue,
Where, with its potent and imperious mood,
   Youth's instant immortality does make
   Mock of Time's wisdom and his lengthened ache.

LV.

By the moon's sickle swiftly harvested
Now do the thick-sown growths of heaven fall,
Now distantly the few, large stars are spread,
Mute, mute, but dangerous in each interval ;
By the moon's magic now the earth is held,
By magic and the white eclipse of May,
And I, too, captive to the cirque compelled,
Push the tinged lilacs from my door away.
The shrub-set lawns, the denser shadowed hedge,
The vine-masked porches, and the glittering street,
Open before me, but my soul is pledge
That the whole world lies naked at my feet.
   On the next slope Endymion sleeps in trance,
   And O, the wind whispers deliverance.

LVI.

Away! They wait me on those upper lawns
(Where the broad chestnut and the sweeping fir
Shadow the slumber of the undying fawns)
They wait me whom the god has set astir,—
The leaf-crowned, thrysus-sceptred god, who late
Rode through this village at the heels of Spring,
And left the young men's footsteps more elate.
And set the maidens' heads a-mutinying;
Who now by forceful summoning does sway
Youths, maidens, to his woodland revel loose,
Each with a branch of ivy for the pay
Of the great Master of the feast they choose;
    And I, too, go where showering snows of light
    Sift through dark roofs to mask the road's steep flight.

LVII.

The altar burns, the wine is broached, and now
One by one from the thick-stemmed forest comes
The happy company of the ivy bough,
And the flutes greet us, and the fiercer drums :
Askance we gaze, but the deep god, who stands
Gold-ruddy in the moonlight's faded flame,
Soothes all our shyness into happy bands
And sets a new stain on the cheek of shame.
I close my eyes and open them again.
Still stays the Vision, the Enchanter stays,
Stay the lolled figures of his Mænad train,
The leaf-wound thrysi and the altar's blaze,
 White-statued maidens and bronze-burnished men,
 Moonlight and midnight, and the mountain glen.

LVIII.

Still stay they : but the smiling Master lifts
His thrysus and a phantom vividwise
(Moon-brightening all the circle-heaped drifts)
Stands in the middle of our mysteries.
O flowing limbs, or free or clad in white !
O darker lordship of the daring head !
O lips ! O eyes ! O clear and matchless might !
Madness my gain is or thy sacred bed.
About us many figures move and float,
The guests of Bacchus break into a dance,
The silver flutes of heaven sound remote,
And nearer is the Mænad dissonance :
    This, the most perfect night's most perfect hour
    Opens, and opens the woods' inmost bower.

LIX.

Hark ! hark ! Below girl-voices echo, singing
A ditty of the rose and revel time :
" Hymen, O Hymen hither we are bringing,
Hard is the way and difficult to climb :
Hymen we bring but struggle to delay her,
A woodland estray innocent of men,
Fain would she bless, but will not we obey her,
Moonlight made girls cold in this forest glen :
Why should we hurry to that hushèd chamber
Where waits the bridegroom red and pale by turn ?
Without, the dew lies cool where roses clamber,
Within, the torches and the faces burn.
 Passion we fear, passion that slays the dream
 Born of the fugitive, faint moonlight gleam."

LX.

The work is done : the Master has withdrawn
His purple-splashed and silver-painted crew ;
Gone is the glade, the oak-trees gone, and gone
The stars' intruding figures out of view ;
And lo ! the wonder-phantom at my side,
With arm moon-dyed, rose-fragrant, and with breast
Tumultuous movèd as the plunging tide,
Turns in the darkness as to seek the rest.
Now is my being shaken to the root ;
Now would I cry, kneel, grovel in my fears ;
But my blood urges on a stronger suit,
To conquer, conquer for all coming years ;
    And in this night of passion does the Shape
    Grow real, and no longer seek escape.

LXI.

I wake and leaning on my arm behold
The morning remnant of the gods' wild flight,
The panther skins, the sleeping Shape of gold,
Winged Hope made certain in a single night.
Under the branches of the tree of Jove,
Sure to my touch and glorious in my eyes,
The creature and incarnate soul of Love
Lies in the proof of all my phantasies.
This is the neck whose turning thrilled me, this
The arm that maddened, this the blinding hair ;
Here are the thousand presences of bliss ;
Eyes that make mine what mocking lips misswear.
    Now for my thought, my freedom, no regret ;
    He whom Love has o'erthrown lives prouder yet.

LXII.

Desire has touched me with its rod divine,
Straight and aspiring stand I, and my heart,
Full of the larger graces libertine,
Scorns its old ways and low-contented part.
We pass the forest threshold, and our shades
Enter the world before us, to possess
Whatever glory equals, nor upbraids
Our high-exampled bliss and blessedness.
Love's profuse and uncalculated joy
Demands from life an answering expense,
Purple that fades not, gold without alloy,
All perfect and all pure magnificence.
    The body's splendor and the spirit's ease,
    All my security I build on these.

LXIII.

Then do I fall on rumor and renown ;
For Love is not content in its own sphere
To live and lighten, but far up and down
Unto all other orbits must appear.
Therefore I take the pipe wherein is bound
The strain of Orpheus, or what later notes
Drew the immortals unto Grecian ground,
And on the air anew the anguish floats ;
Or stung to action by the fading Wreath
I seize a sword, and where the battle swarms
Move through the ranks of onset, move to death,
Move with the glitter of the goddess's arms ;—
   So Love more deep may love my absent face,
   So that renown may hover round my race.

LXIV.

Yet Peace in some walled garden close were best,
Peace not o'erleaping or burst in upon,
With Innocence for a perpetual guest,
All effort made and every guerdon won.
Pure airs are here, untainted springs abound,
Filtered through earthy channels from the sky,
And in and out the rose-disordered ground
Sweet and familiar figures wander by.
But the more high, distinct, and awful race,
The brood of glory in their woe intense,
They by report but enter in this place,
As stars they move us, but their march is hence.
   Here is my cloistered seat, here have I known
   Hope's twentieth restoration to her throne.

LXV.

Him do I praise, who, plunging in the wave,
Wrestles one bout with the frame-crushing coil,
Then, with some quick-snatched treasure, seeks his cave,
Lurèd no longer by the ocean-spoil ;
Him do I praise, who, striking in the throng
Of athletes, is the equal of their day,
But leaves unclaimed the crown that should belong
To the swift-running feet or muscles' play ;
Him do I praise, who, safe with wife and child,
Safe by the oak-fire to his hearth-gods made,
Frames a clear music from earth's outcry wild,
Seeking no other audience and no aid,
    Virtue I praise and not its act or praise,
    The soul's true centre, not the circle rays.

LXVI.

Ay, let the world retake the gifts it gave,—
Ease, honor, all its fair-disguisèd harms ;
I am content if Love but stay, and have
My world within the rondure of her arms :
Condemned unto no business but to buy
Kisses with kisses, to heap joys amain,—
This is the merriest kind of beggary ;
Merchants may envy my quick-counted gain.
Ah, what a weary travel is our act,—
Here, there, and back again to seek some prize ;
Friends who are wise their voyage do contract
To the safe path between each other's eyes.

    Come, my sweet mistress, love shall life outlast ;
    Let the world drift, for we are anchored fast.

LXVII.

Ah, the forgotten spell upon me comes,
The circle I evaded closes in,
The angry Genius lifts its head and roams
Through the fair paradise I hoped to win !
At talk, at feast, at play perchance I sit
Close-shut with Love, but still a darker third
Enters the place, and She and I and It,
Chilled, fall apart and speak no other word.
Then beauty seems to fade from Beauty's face,
Ay, from my side, Love, darkening, seems to flow,
Far, far removed from its wonted place.
From my heart's throne her mirrored self does go,
    And undisguised the Dæmon there again
    Smiles at the opening of his sterner reign.

LXVIII.

Dimness, cool rest, and dreams within,—without
The echo-deafened, lapsèd monotone
And glare of noontide. O, let Love not doubt
That forfeit in me which the world does share
Though drawn, I gaze upon the whirlpool track
Under the window. Madness, rage, is there,
And battle ever, though Peace does not lack
Prospect of fields serene and kindly air ;
Throngs meet and melt, fates alter ere you mark :
There goes a funeral, here a new-made wife,
Rich harvest-wains move laboring by,—but hark !
Up from the peace, this tumult, this rich life,
   Up from the street is flung the self-same cry
   Wrenched from thy marble lips, Philosophy !

LXIX.

Love sleeps! Her limbs are charmèd in their flow,
Bronze-buried is her bosom in her hair,
Flushed, fragrant like the Springtide's second snow,
Fruit is in promise, and the bloom is there.
God! and must these calm limbs, with convulsed stress,
Fester to earth? Must this hair's glory fade?
Must these lips leave the roses rivalless?
Against perfection is a canon made?
Kisses to stay the ruin! No, my heart:
Thy kisses and thy tears alike would burn,
An iron anger is thy only part;
Back, back unto thy desolation turn.
   What matters it? Antigone is dead,
   And Juliet keeps for aye her wormy bed.

LXX.

Love unashamed, Love undishonored,
Love of the lineage or the life of fire,
Love with the burning limbs, the golden head,
The glittering weapons, and the godlike ire,
Love has departed, but her shadow stays,
A ghost of sunlight whitely glimmering by,
A smoke-wreath from a too quick quenched blaze,
A ruin that we name satiety.
Though to her touch the last nerve quivers still,
Though the eye makes account of all her charms,
The soul's gates open not nor ever will,
Save tyrant-like she shake them with her arms :
    Love must train eagles and discard her doves,
    And for armed camps desert her moonlit groves.

LXXI.

Cannot thy lips, Love, take the graver's cast
To make their thick-strown seals the impress of fate?
Can'st thou not cease to alter and stay fast
At thy orbed noon and ardor passionate?
Can'st thou not burst the barrier and defense
'Twixt thee and me, that to our strong desire
Thought may be one with thought and sense with sense
Inseparable as a single fire?
Can'st thou not order that within the heart
Degree and doubt shall cease their dangerous plea?
No, and thrice no! Then let us kiss and part;
Strange or indifferent must our beings be.
   Soul-suicide am I that banish Love,
   But the dark stirs with life, and there I move.

LXXII.

Come, mourners, to the funeral of Love !
Come thou bright day-god, come Night's argent spouse,
Ye diverse-colored creatures cloud-inwove,
Ye gleamy pageants of the forest boughs !
Bring the clear-tinted, virgin buds of Spring,
Bring June's mid-rose-day's myriad perfumes,
Autumn's thick-fallen, deadening foliage bring,
To bury deep the Lord of earthy dooms.
And let that solemn chantry of the woods,
From whose winged priests perpetual requiems rise,
Loose all its voices and their echoing floods,
To sound Love's sad, religious obsequies.
   So do your service—and when ye are gone
   There's time enough for Life and me to mourn.

LXXIII.

But we are left, O Dæmon ; we endure,
Though each lamenting echo be a blow,
Thou dost deny me happiness ; be sure
Thou not refusest the boon : To know ! To know !
Not by slight guesses may I now be won,
Dream's faith would question if faith aught could lack,
Thou must voyage with me to the central One,
Mine be the peril, mine the journey back.
Thou hast been judge of me and still would press
Thy service for each errand of the soul.
Now o'er thee rises a ruler merciless ;
Thou must be all, do all, and all control.
    Love, Joy, Hope went for that thou didst insist ;
    Now find a worthier for each friend dismissed.

LXXIV.

Come, let us hence, ere we are grown too weak !
An immortal charge of sorrow have we gained ;
Twinned now in hate together must we seek
The isolation that before we feigned.
The gates of life close on us, clanging wrath,
Their towers are sentineled to do us wrong ;
That way again we go not ; here's our path ;
The chill of space strikes on us ; we are strong.
Ay, we are strong, and free to choose our world
Out of yon streaming drift of ceaseless stars :
But hold !   This sere thing on my shoulder curled—
Autumn's last gift ere we had crossed earth's bars—
   O'erweights me till I stagger.   One frail leaf
   Crushes me with the whole world's woe and grief.

LXXV.

The mighty soul that is ambition's mate,
Tied to the shiftings of a certain star,
Forgets the circle of its mortal state
And what its planetary aspects are ;
Till, in conjunctive course and wandering,
Out of its trance and treasure-dream of hope
It wakens, poor illusionary thing,
Wingless, without desire, or deed, or scope.
So have I with imaginations played
Till I have lost life's sure and single good,
Forgotten friendships, broken vows, and made
My heart a highway for ingratitude.
   And, driven to the desert of the sky,
   Fear now no thing but immortality.

LXXVI.

Worlds are our quest.   Dæmon, thine errand try.

Knock at this gate !   Here lives no doubt or woe.

Be answered !   Hark !   That anguished, mortal cry !

God, do they sentinel thy heavens so ?

Another star !   Haunt this of serene joys,

Content's fair harbor.   Lo, the doors roll wide :

Two giant figures struggling, and a voice,—

" Pass, for we die as all our fathers died ! "

A third world then ! Knock ! Question !—all is known,

All fathomed here.   So !   Comes the answer back,—

" We know the footing safe that falls on stone ;

But tread beyond, the path may something lack."

    What is our voyage worth, O Dæmon ?   We

    Had yesterday more than this history.

LXXVII.

Through vault to vault we move, from dome to dome,
Above unfathomably mirroring floors,
Nor to the limit darkness can we come,
Though chaos in the heart beat out its wars.
No secret do the stars yield, nor the air
Where the leagued beacon-runners leap and burn.
Whence are their fires? What message do they bear?
Hopeless the soul looks forth and does return.
But thou, O Dæmon, can'st put out thy hand,
And one by one these lights do sweep from space,
As runners at the word dart from their stand,
And silence waits the issue of the race.
  The abyss is ours; thoughts circle and its throne,
  And for the end we wait, and wait alone.

LXXVIII.

Thought, only thought, a darkness and a blank,
Groping we stir, lost in the empty void ;
Blotted the awful heavens rank o'er rank,
Barrèd the prison of the soul decoyed.
No living presence here may force its aid,
No echo of delivery or of doom,
No dream may come to soothe, for dreams are made
The second circle of these walls of gloom.
Terror alone keeps with us cold and chill,
Constant before the closèd eyes that see,
Terror and the immitigable Will
Which moves not, acts not, but must ever be.
So wait we for the secret long desired :
Others have failed for that they feared or tired.

LXXIX.

I light one torch and fling it in the dark ;
Fire-tapestried on night or shadow cast,
A thousand forms lit by that little spark
In endless rush and whirl go eddying past.
Again a torch and all are gone, save they,
Time, Space, and that unfathomable One,
Oblivion's rival, whom the rest obey,
Yet from Oblivion's self have never known.
Soul, make thy choice ! Either be of the throng
That dies in birth and has no self-control,
Or to the pure and secret force belong,
The soundless dark that orbs the perfect Whole ;
    Either abide in change and restless flame,
    Or in the nothing whence thy being came.

LXXX.

Dæmon, O guide, is there no third way ope,
May we not 'scape that whirlpool, this abyss ?
Delusions can'st thou give, and give me hope,
But Death thy only certain answer is.
Sadly thou turnest thy unavailing eyes
On mine and like two mirrors opposite,
Emptiness unto emptiness replies :
O thy conception was the womb of night,
No stars did presage or look on thy birth,
The Real Image came not where thou layest,
Pinioned, thou darest to judge of freedom's worth,
And islanded to know the ocean-waste.
    Thought cannot govern what it has not gained,
    Nor measure God in whom it is contained.

LXXXI.

But I do know, and am at far remove,
One with some spirit of universal sway,
And, but for thy most busy aid, might prove
Lord over elements I now obey.
A power is in me, but whene'er I seek,
Thy face is all I see.   Thou dost intrude
Thy dominoed figure, infinite, unique,
Masking all else in thine own multitude ;
Thou dost so order it within my house
That thou art all the entertainment there,—
The wine, the food, the fire, the host, the spouse ;
Thou art the very guests whom thou biddest fair.
    Naught can escape thee, nothing shroud in gloom,
    No unknown figure rise to work thy doom.

LXXXII.

Yet, spite thy inquisition, still there lurks
Some trembling motion in my heart's hid shrine ;
Lo ! the miraculous symbol lives and works, —
Daylight is drownèd in a glow divine.
New purged, my eyes see the new glory there, —
Creatures who dwelt without my former sense,
The under valleys of the smoothèd air,
Stars that were dark in whirling march intense.
Now the thought needs not seek for the abyss,
The world's great circle that does still retreat ;
Near, near at hand, at every turning, this
Yawns, and a bridge falls o'er it to my feet,
   And ere the pathway half is overtrod
   Rises on me the final Dawn of God.

LXXXIII.

Mine eyes fall from the statue to the plinth,
Back unto sense and thought and sense I sink,
Back to the windings of the labyrinth,
Back to the old question and the broken link.
Ah, I must cease to struggle, and accept
The iron limits of my prison-place,
Remit the knightly vigil I have kept,
And swear a truce out with the dark and base;
And thou, O inward singer, who with me
Kept the thronged strait of fight against all odds,
Done is thy song and sword-play! Banished be
Pipe to the hierarchies of buried gods!
    This is our lesson, that the spirit came
    Out of the whirl it now essays to name.

LXXXIV.

Then fails our hope.   Despair is all of life ;
Evil has Good's most gentle smile in use,
And Good does borrow Evil's bloody knife ;
Either is excellent, and none may choose.
Base and ignoble did the soul begin,
No path was pointed it, no goal was placed ;
Blind, in the dark, a race it went to win,
Guideless without, and its ownself a waste.
No race it wins if day and night be one,
If the great forms of Law and ends of Good
Live not for it to make comparison ;
No race it wins, but jostles in a wood.
    Save that God separate stands, creation must
    Die beyond death and crumble past all dust.

LXXXV.

Thou livest, O soul ! be sure, though earth be flames,
Though lost be all the paths the planets trod,
Thou hast not aught to do with signs and names,
With Life's false art or Time's brief period.
Thy being wast ere yet the heavens were not,
Gently thy breath the waves of ether stirred,
And often hast thou feared and oft forgot,
Yet knew thyself when rang the parent Word.
Long hast thou played at change through chain on chain
Of beings, drooping now in strange descent,
Now adding bloom to bloom and beauty's gain,
Through subtle growths of glory evident.
    O earnest play, thyself apart oft smilest,
    One still at heart, that so thyself beguilest.

LXXXVI.

Perchance, my Dæmon, thou and I alone
Have the inheritance of this changing flow,
Whose lapse leaves nothing certain, nothing known ;
Perchance the figure and the dream of show
Are but the blazon on the gates of fate
That close upon us wheresoe'er we turn,
Upon whose lucid darkness iterate
Our myriad, mirroring echoes live and burn.
So we but move, and suns remote arise ;
So we but speak, and stars chime in accord ;
So we but think, and breed vast phantasies,
Delusions that do dominate their lord ;
   So we but knock, and thereupon will be
   God's thunder moving through eternity.

LXXXVII.

False fiend, this is the cunning of thine art !
What were truth worth if mine own thought were truth
What were life worth to the void-wheeling heart ?
No ! by the altars of the gods of youth ;
No ! by the hill-fires of the rising sun ;
No ! by the smoking incense of the sea,—
Life's blazing circle round me still must run,
Nor I from it nor it can go from me.
Yet dwells one power aloof from life, to whom
Fate is not fate, who works not for increase,
Who lays no hand upon the whirring loom,
Whose action is what silence dreams of peace ;
 And my glory is that not the great world's light
 Obscures from me this deeper infinite.

LXXXVIII.

Again a guess! The dicing moon below
With its cloud-shadows on gray slopes may glance ;—
May not the soul, as idle-eager, throw
One and another and another chance ?
Is it not true, is it not true that He
Who from perfection stooped to halting act,
Who from Himself did form His enemy,
Who put in question what He had not lacked,
Fashioned as well the soul of man, to have
Part in the riot and ruin, yet to bear
A higher touch, indomitably brave,
Wings that should weary down the wildest air,
    Eyes that should see where light itself does end,
    Courage to still attack and still defend ?

LXXXIX.

Come to a truce, my thought, let us be friends !
Why should I quarrel that thou can'st not know
The all in all, the space wherein space ends,
Where I have been but thou can'st never go ?
Praise, praise to thee for that thou keepest the fames
Of all the shadowy godheads of the earth ;
Praise that thou oft repeatest more sacred names
Whose echo in the world has little worth.
"Wisdom " thou criest, though all thy way be dark ;
" Justice " thou callest, though evil walls thee round ;
" Love, love," thou singest, and soarest ere thou mark
If any daylight calls thee from the ground.
    Truth's veil thou knowest, and, ah ! more wisely fond,
    Thou knowest thou dost not know what lies beyond.

XC.

Thus dost thou speak : " Master, I can no more ;
No nimbler herald had the gods. Here, there,
About thy prison have I sought the door ;
My plumes are broken and my eyes despair.
Let divine reason yield to brutish sway,
Cease to perplex the riddle with thy wit,
Beloved oblivion seek some lower way,
Since mounting wings will no wise compass it.
Fall ! for the air is fatal where thou art ;
Sleep ! for with spectres is the sunlight rife ;
Forget ! forget ! forget ! and free the heart
From the iron leaguer of its foes of life."
    So : and I take, obedient to thy voice,
      Lethe's black draught and the ignobler choice.

XCI.

But thence is madness ! I could never stay
Lost, that once had the action of a star ;
Necessity is on me to o'ersway
And sweep from darkness proud and regular !
But madness is thy aim. Thou wouldst arrange
A halting-place where Hope and Act may meet
And neither know the other's awful change.
Then is my throne become Orestes' seat,
And for the stand at bay 'gainst hounds of pain
I take a vacant gaze and huddled state,
And the snakes glide and glitter in my brain.
No, Dæmon, not that way to baffle Fate.
    Though all God's judgment in one word is loosed,
    Still would I answer, though the sole accused.

XCII.

Where sleeps the Origin thy power dost pine ;
Thou dwindlest as we near the obscure brink,
Thou by my sufferance livest, not I by thine,
For I can think or can disdain to think.
In the old days thou madest divorce and pain
'Twixt the proud world of shadows and myself ;
As great a gulf now yawns to part us twain,
Severed we gaze each from his dizzy shelf.
Mummer of masks, subtly thou madest report—
Potent o'er changes which did live in thee—
Of the world's doing, and didst still distort
And barrier truth without from truth in me.
    Now on this jut of space where we have flown
    Unmask ! Be true ! Be as thou art ! Be known !

XCIII.

Horror! The last disguise from off thee slips,
Threatening I know my new antagonist,
The fiend that companied me into eclipse
Gave me his torch, but all lights else dismissed;
Death's lineaments thou hast, but yet art like
My inmost being. O immortal thief,
Thou heldst my citadel wherefrom to strike
Hope from my soul, and every starred belief!
Now must we part! Ay, do thy worst! Uptear
My rooted laws of being and of life,
Obliterate all the divine dreams that were,
Open the door where chaos rolls its strife;—
   Thou keep'st me not. Nobly thy prisoner
   Ends my parole, and lo! my camp's astir.

XCIV.

Be then, O beautiful yet sombre one,
Hostile or neuter to my haughtly soul,
Traitor that deemedst I could not live alone,
Tutored and tethered by the mind's control,
Thought's not the soul, though the great officer
That does its captain threat by its retreat,
But Death withdraws, and Doubt does with thee spur,
And the soul rises conquering and complete.
Sunlight in sunlight, cloud in the obscure,
Oblivion's living essence float I free,
A restless point of life that must endure,
A fire that shall outwatch eternity.
    Proud was I, Thought, clad forth in thy array,
    But now I know thy garments were decay.

XCV.

Yet all the glory that thine hour did give,
Thrillèd I feel, all thy creations past,—
Less than divine, for all were fugitive ;
Thy shows did waver while my soul stood fast.
And oft the cost of parting do I count
That leaves me beggared as my voyage begins,
For past thy empire my amassed amount
Uncurrent is, and no step forward wins.
Yet can I go no farther by thy side,
Not though thy treaty is to hold me free,
Not though thou chain all Nature for my pride,
Not though life's secret shall no secret be,
    Not though the cheat is nobly not to die,
    For not to live in splendor will I lie.

XCVI.

I take a trumpet, for no thing less proud
May sound thy dirge, O proud and mighty Thought.
Thou at the last to Fate's array hast bowed ;
Conquerer till now, this field thou leavest unfought ;
But thy great figure fills the slopes of time ;
Where ocean ebbs into night's orb, where drawn
The hostile stars are glittering, where upclimb
The red and splendid shadows of the dawn,
There dost thou glide, and the exultant cry,
Creation's word, leaps from thy lips ; but now,
Master of the divided mystery,
Now dost thou let the world obliterate flow
    In darkness,—all the power and pomp it gave
    Dead ! and sunk with thee in one common grave.

XCVII.

Myself am me, though darkness girds me round,
Ay, though death makes its seat within my heart ;
Pure leaps the flame, clear rings the crystal sound,
That to the Whole reverbs my deathless Part ;
Though a thin ghost through aisles of chance I glide,
Nothing of alms will I solicit there ;
Though Faith would warm me at her breathing side,
And Hope apparel with her roseate air.
I have relinquished all such trivial things
That in the count of glory once were great :
They last not, they reveal not hidden springs,
No piecemeal keys unseal the doors of fate.
   Naked to these I come, not clad in dust,
   And they shall shudder as my spirit must.

XCVIII.

Courage, the one sole virtue that I bear
Through my long voyage and continuance ;
Courage, the rebel that would claim or share
The kingdom aimed at both Fate and Chance,—
Courage still keeps my soul.   The days dismissed
Pass noiseless by me that were noisy once,
The central flame of all fades like a mist,
At its last ebb the tide of nature runs,
And the great world of dream, built in the mind,
Based beyond ruin by time's ebb and flow,
A citadel within the deaf and blind,
Loosens its sure foundations and does go.
　　Still courage keeps my soul.   'Though baffled, this
　　Broods like an eagle o'er the blank abyss.

XCIX.

O eagle, flown beyond this faded day,
Thy height is won, thou hast thine heart's desire ;
A wider ether would thy wings essay,
And the fire in thee sought the source of fire.
Now is the end, now night thy gaze restrainest,
On vacant space thy plumes can beat no more,
Beyond thou canst not, and beneath disdainest,
Thou hold'st devoured the deeps thou hast passed o'er.
What is there left ?   In narrow circles flying,
To wheel forever on this verge of life,
Or solemn-souled and sure, and fate defying,
Sweep in proud splendor past the shores of strife,
   Ages on ages hence perchance to fall,
   Or to make covert and discover all.

C.

TO MY MOTHER.

Adieu and dedication, the twin gates
That close and ope the avenue of song,
Here at one bound I set ; and the dread Fates
Woo to rest here and stay the eternal wrong.
Adieu, my dark Familiar and his quest !
Adieu, adieu my dreams ! but unto thee,
Who art more noble than the Fancy's best,
Let greeting and let recantation be.
My doubt, my embittered thought, thou shamest, with old
And sweet content, and thy time-yellowed hair
Makes true the heroic fables we are told,
Makes all the train of womanhood seem fair.
   Much do I lack, yet count I honor won,
   Or fortune, less than that I am thy son.

www.ingramcontent.com/pod-product-compliance
Lightning Source LLC
Chambersburg PA
CBHW032154010726
47493CB00008BA/2693